# JORDAN BYRD'S
# COURAGE TO SOAR

## ATHLETE ADVENTURERS

# JORDAN BYRD'S COURAGE TO SOAR

## SPECIAL THANKS

### NICOLE BEDFORD

# JORDAN BYRD'S COURAGE TO SOAR

## CHAPTERS

Meet Jordan, a young boy
with big dreams. He loves
to run track and play football.

Jordan looks up to his older sister Brittany, who is a star athlete. Jordan dreams of being just like her and winning championships.

One day, Jordan was feeling sad and unmotivated. He was struggling with his athletic abilities and felt like giving up on his dreams. Just then, a colorful bird flew down and landed on his shoulder.

The bird introduced itself as
Sky, and promised to help
Jordan achieve his goals.

Sky took Jordan on an incredible adventure through mountains, forests, and rivers.

S

K

Y

Along the way, Jordan
faced many challenges,
but Sky encouraged him
to keep going and never
give up. Jordan learned that
with hard work and
determination,
anything is possible.

As they journeyed, Jordan began to see improvements in his athletic abilities. He ran faster and threw farther than ever before.

He realized that he was capable of achieving his dreams if he kept pushing himself.

One day, Jordan and Sky came across a group of athletes who were training for a big championship. Jordan recognized them as some of the best athletes in the world.

He felt intimidated and
unsure of himself, but
Sky reminded him that he
had the talent and
determination to be great.
One push-up at a time!

Finally, the day of the
championship arrived.
Jordan was nervous but
excited to showcase his
skills.
He ran as fast as he could,
threw the ball as far as
possible, and never gave
up, even when he fell behind.

In the end, Jordan won the championship, just like he had always dreamed of.

From that day forward,
Jordan knew that he
could achieve anything he
wanted, as long as he put
in the effort and never
gave up.
Later in life, Jordan went
on to play football at
San Diego State
and the NFL!

Jordan hopes everyone
learns to dream for the sky!

Made in the USA
Columbia, SC
05 December 2023

27849030R00018